The Pha

An Adventure Ghost Story

Irvine Hunt

by Irvine Hunt

To Sheila
with the
author's
Best wishes

Irvine

For four loved ones, Gwyn and Maisie
and Shiloh and Christian

Published by Bishop Pot Press, Cumbria

E-book format:
978-0-9575338-7-5

Print-on-Demand paperback:
978-1-5171301-8-2

Kim Lewis designed and created the cover (kim.lurati@gmail.com)
Edited by Georgia Laval (www.lavalediting.co.uk)

A crossover novel.

All characters are the work of the writer's imagination and any resemblance to real persons, alive or dead, is purely coincidental.

Other Books by Irvine Hunt

Print editions
- *The Drover's Boy*, an adventure novel, Handstand Press
- *The Ghost Show*, an adventure novel (follow-up to *The Drover's Boy*), Handstand Press
- *Norman Nicholson's Lakeland: A Prose Anthology*, Robert Hale
- *Manlaff and Toewoman*, poems, Rusland Press

E-book editions
- *Wild Runaways*, an adventure novel

- *Dating the Witch*, short stories

- *Cub Reporter: The Accrington Observer*, autobiographical

- *A Young Man Afoot*, a travel memoir

CONTENTS

About the Author

Another thanks

For all the help... thank you again to Ross and Josie Baxter, Sheelagh Ellwood, Fiona Cox, Paul Mellor, Liz Nuttall, Liz Stannard, skilled editor Georgia Laval, computer expert Andrew Ward, artist Kim Lewis who soon sensed more in the story than I did... and to Shiloh Fetzek, who thankfully kept the tale on the right track.

1 – THE FACE

ALISON came to a halt at the edge of the pond and glanced back at the farmhouse. Satisfied she was not being watched she hitched her jeans, turned to the water and began to pull up the irises.

She worked quickly, throwing the plants onto the ground behind her, knowing that Aunt Dado would soon come out and would want to know what was going on.

Strictly speaking Cobbles Farm was no longer a farm. Strongly built of stone and slate, it stood alone in the fields at the end of a rough track. The cattle and the sheep had gone. The corrugated iron sheds had gone. Doors and windows had been painted, and now, of all things, Alison's guardian, Dado, was insisting it was to be called a *private house*. Not only that, she seemed to be planning even more changes.

Well she just would, thought Alison, who had loved the old building the way it used to be, faded and a bit untidy.

Throughout all the changes the pond shone under the sky like a beautiful mirror, concealing its secret.

Alison soon made a good wide gap through to open water. It was June and the thick band of irises encircled the pond like a green and yellow crown. But that was the trouble; tall and beautiful though they were, there were too many.

She squatted on a boulder. During all the unhappiness this had been a favourite corner, though gradually it had become overgrown, mostly with irises. Now that she was clearing them away it was beginning to look good again.

A moorhen clucked and moved in among the stems. Tomorrow she would widen the gap.

Alison sat forward a little as she noticed a whitish patch in the water. She hadn't seen it before. She stood up to get a better view and it took her a moment to realize what it was.

"Alison! When are you going to come in?"

Dado's stocky figure was at the farmhouse door, tying back her long grey hair. "I want help with the supper. I want an early night!"

But Alison stood at the edge of the pond, suddenly numb. In the water a face was staring up at her.

Dado came across. "What's the matter with you, child? And what's this mess? Who told you to pull up all these plants?"

"Aunt D, *look*!"

The face seemed to be drifting alongside the stems.

"Someone's in the water!"

"What?"

Dado stared but saw nothing. "Don't be silly. Come inside and get the table set. I'm not doing it all by myself."

"But aunt, there *is*!"

Alison's voice rose.

Dado frowned and started to move away, but a flicker of the light made her pause.

Alison pointed at the patch. It was suddenly much clearer. "It's a girl! Like me!"

Dado held aside a cluster of irises to get a better look, but knew well enough there was nothing to see. "Nonsense. You're as bad as your parents with your silly ideas."

"Mum and Dad weren't bad," said Alison angrily. "And they weren't silly."

Ignoring her protest, Dado steered her back to the house. "Make sure you clear up all the plants. You're always making the place untidy."

Alison's mind was in turmoil. There *was* a girl. She was sure there was. She must give Dado the slip. She had to get back out again!

2 – SEIZED!

But all evening Alison was hemmed in. One way or another Dado did not allow her a free moment. First, help to get the supper, then the dishes to be washed; after that, maddeningly, homework. Why hadn't she done it sooner?

She struggled through a stream of long divisions. Despairingly, she realised there was no way she was going to get out to the pond again that night. Dado was watching her too closely.

At last her homework was done.

"Now give your shoes a clean, and do brush your hair will you?"

"My shoes *are* clean!"

They weren't and Alison knew it. And she *liked* her hair wild: it made her feel free. Dado did keep going on. Well, she'd show her.

She retreated to the pantry and sat on a stool and tried not to think about the face in the water. Rebelliously, she polished her black shoes with brown polish. Dado's anger when she saw them would be worth it.

Ten o'clock was striking before Alison went to bed. She lay awake as she tried to remember the face. It had almost seemed *alive*, yet she knew it couldn't be. She must get out early in the morning.

An age passed before she fell asleep but it was daylight when she woke. She scrambled out of bed and ran to the window.

Too late: she heard Dado's bedroom door open. Dressing quickly, she put on her lucky amber necklace and immediately felt better. It had been her mother's favourite piece of jewellery.

Dado came out of the bathroom. "Goodness, you are up early. In that case you can get your own breakfast, and make sure you clean away the dishes."

"I will," said Alison.

"And leave plenty of time to get the school bus. You'll fall one of these days, always racing up the track."

"I'll go out the front door. It's quicker."

"No you won't! You'll go out at the back, and stay away from the water. I won't pull you out if you fall in."

"Aunt D – I'm *twelve* now."

Why did Dado carry on? Why wasn't she more like Aunt Betty, Alison's favourite aunt? To be fair, she had heard that Dado had lost her own parents when she was young. Perhaps it was true. Like me, she thought. She remembered the day her mother and father were in a car accident. She had been at home with Dado while her parents had been out shopping. It all seemed long ago now, but it still hurt. A policeman had come to the door and told them what had happened.

*

Dado tutted impatiently as Alison grabbed her school satchel. She hadn't noticed the shoes – her mind was on something else.

"While I think about it, I'm going to take down some of these pictures. There are far too many."

Alison could hardly believe what her aunt was saying. "But they were Mum's and Dad's!"

Her father and mother had both been artists and the house was full of their paintings. Portraits of friends, and billowing cloud scenes, dogs and shepherds, farmyard cats with their tails curled, trees, misty hills…

But Dado was in an organising mood. "I'm sorry, all they do is collect dust, and really no one looks at them any more."

"They do! *I* do," protested Alison. "Don't take them down Aunt D. *Please.*"

Dado smiled faintly. She had anticipated that Alison would object. "You needn't worry, I'll not throw any away. They can go into the studio at the barn end. But I'll leave the ones in the hallway if that makes you feel any better."

Alison eyed her aunt. The hallway pictures were all family portraits dominated by the whiskered face of Alison's grandfather. He too had been an artist. She guessed now that Dado would take down his picture in time. Ever since she had become Alison's guardian Dado seemed to enjoy changing things.

Dismally, Alison trudged up the track. Desperate though she was to go across to the pond, she knew she dared not. She could feel her aunt's eyes pinned on her. Later she would definitely look; it was Monday and Dado would be in town collecting her pension and shopping. If all went well, once school was over Alison knew she would have an hour at home to herself. Well, that at least would be good.

Despite this thought, a bad day followed. Maths again. Alison was nearly good at maths. Nearly. Others in the class were brilliant.

I'm better with words, she reminded herself.

And then, remembering the pond, she felt she must have been mistaken. *I'm being stupid. It was just a reflection. It was probably an empty fertiliser bag blown in off the fields. That had happened before.*

She was first to get onto the school bus and sat hunched up all the way home, willing it to go faster.

At last she raced down to the pond and even before she reached the water's edge she could see the white patch.

She took a deep breath and halted abruptly, her heart pounding. It really *was* a girl. The same girl. And the girl's face was alive! It was! It was!

Trying not to tremble, she knelt on the bank. The flickering image was closer in than yesterday. Holding her breath, Alison reached out as if to touch it with the tips of her fingers.

A hand slid up out of the water and took hold of hers.

Alison screamed.

3 – ALICIA

At once the hand tightened its grip and for a terrifying moment Alison thought she was going to be dragged into the water.

But the opposite happened.

She tumbled back onto the grass as the girl rose out of the pond, water pouring from her clothes. Shocked, Alison scrambled to her feet.

The girl looked about her own age, but while Alison's hair was fair and wild, the strange girl's hair was black and cropped short. She stood unsmiling and bare footed as Alison stared at her sodden dress. It was dark and rough, almost coarsely woven.

For moments they said nothing, then Alison could stand it no longer and broke the silence: "W-who are you?"

The girl did not answer.

"C-can't you speak?" asked Alison.

Still the girl remained silent.

Alison realised they had let go of one another's hands. She was still trembling.

The girl stared, unblinking, water dripping from her clothes.

"You must be able to talk?"

The girl's eyes flickered. Her lips opened. There was a long pause, then she uttered a half-heard word: "Y-e-e-e-s."

It was a strange, ill-formed sound, long and drawn out. She spoke faintly, as if the word had been hauled into the present from far away.

Slowly moving a hand, Alison pointed at herself and then at the farmhouse behind her. "This is where I live."

Again the girl's eyes flickered. Her lips parted: "You are Al-is-on," she said.

Alison was shocked. Who had told the girl her name? Who was she?

"I have wait-ed," said the girl.

She looked solemn, her face white.

"What do you mean?"

"You watch… by the water."

Alison started to speak, then she stopped as the girl made a slight gesture towards the farmhouse.

"The old one… she calls your name."

The old one. That would be Aunt Dado.

She hardly dared to ask her next question.

"The water." She glanced at the glittering surface. "I mean, how long…"

"Very long," said the girl.

"But… why haven't you drowned?"

"Because I don't."

The girl's voice, which at first had been scarcely a whisper, was becoming stronger. Alison stared into her face and saw how smooth it was, almost like porcelain. It was perfect, unblemished, and white, very white. She knew she ought to be scared, but somehow she wasn't.

"I think you are afraid," said the girl.

"No, I'm not!" said Alison quickly. "You made me jump, that's all."

A car was turning off the road. It was Dado!

"Oh, quick, please, won't you tell me your name?"

A flicker of light seemed to encompass the girl.

"It is Alicia."

Alison was astonished. "That's like mine!"

The girl shook her head. "My name is older."

Dado's car was drawing in behind the house.

"Wait!" cried Alison. "What's happening?"

The girl was becoming hazy. She stayed like that for a moment, then she faded abruptly and was no longer there. Shocked, Alison put out a hand as if to touch the empty space. The girl had vanished.

Alison stared at the water, but she was not there either.

Yet the ground was still wet where she had been standing. How could she have vanished?

A crow cawed in the distance. Everything looked normal and ordinary. But Alison felt that everything wasn't ordinary, not any more. She gave a shiver.

4 – LOCKED IN

"Are you coming inside?"

Dado's call brought Alison sharply back to the present. She raced into the house to tell her that no matter what she said, there really *was* a girl in the water.

But her intention was short-lived; a glance at her aunt's tense face changed her mind. Dado was in one of her moods, solid-faced. She waved a hand at the table. "We'll have sausage and mash for supper. It will be quick and easy."

Alison was surprised. "But Aunt D, we had sausages yesterday."

In fact they'd had sausages for two days in a row.

"Well we're going to have them again. And stop calling me Aunt D!"

She banged a frying pan down on the stove.

Alison groaned. She would *turn* into a sausage if they went on like this. Most of the time Dado was all right, but sometimes she wasn't. Today she wasn't.

There was no chance to tell her about the girl.

"I want the meal over with quickly," said Dado severely. "My head is aching and I need an early night. After supper, make sure you do your homework. I don't want another teacher complaining."

Alison sighed. Dado never let her forget. She said things not just once but again and again. Why couldn't Aunt Betty have come to look after her instead of Dado? Aunt B might be scatty but at least she was never grumpy.

When Dado wasn't looking Alison wrapped the biggest sausage in her handkerchief and hid it inside her blouse, but as she rose to clear the dishes she knew instantly it was a mistake, there was a bump.

"What was that?" demanded Dado.

Alison blushed. She scooped up the sausage and put it on her plate. "I was going to eat it later. I'm not hungry."

Dado was angry. "Give that here!"

She grabbed the plate and dropped it with a crash into the sink. "You're becoming a very stupid child. I'm getting tired of your silly behaviour. You act worse than a baby."

That did it. Alison flared. "Thank you! And I'm tired of you, you old cow!"

It came blurting out.

Dado glared, shocked.

Alison raced up the stairs and threw herself onto her bed. How she disliked her aunt! Nothing was ever right!

Moments later she disliked her even more: a rasping click sounded. Alison hurried to the door. It had been locked.

"Let me out!"

She pounded at the wood with her hands.

"I'll break it down!" she yelled.

Of course she knew the door was far too solid.

Angrily she prowled round the room, examining empty cups and plates, leftovers of bedroom snacks. She found what she wanted on the dresser: her penknife.

She flopped back onto her bed. She would wait for the right moment.

*

Nine o'clock was striking before Dado went to bed. Alison waited another half hour then she wiped the penknife's blade on the bedspread. Using the pointed end, she unscrewed the lock and the door swung open.

The landing was in darkness. She fiddled with the screws, replacing them in the holes, and then she tiptoed past Dado's room and went down to the kitchen, intent on sneaking out to the pond. No stupid aunt was going to keep her locked up!

She got no further than opening the back door and immediately had to close it again. Heavy rain was lashing the cobbled yard and hammering the house. Alison groaned. The girl would never be out in this lot!

Resigned, she gave up until tomorrow. Standing on a chair, she pinched a handful of liquorish allsorts from Dado's secret jar, and tiptoed back upstairs.

5 – WHISPERED SECRET

Dado was cool and distant at breakfast. She had fiddled at the lock on Alison's bedroom door seemingly without realising it had already been unlocked.

"Make sure you wash the dishes properly," she ordered.

But Alison was thinking about her rudeness. "Aunt D, I'm sorry about last…"

Dado cut her short. "So you should be."

Alison grabbed her school bag and went out to catch the bus. Sometimes things went wrong and went on staying wrong.

Despite her resolve to keep everything secret, Alison arrived at school bursting to tell someone about the strange girl.

At lunchtime Maddy Vinson came across in the canteen. She was in Alison's class but rarely bothered to talk to her. She was a big girl with streaky blonde hair and well used to getting her own way.

"Listen," said Maddy, sitting alongside. "Did you write up your English? You did? Then lend me your notes. I didn't have time to do mine."

Alison sighed and handed them over. "Don't make it look like you copied. You know Miss M can tell."

"Course not. But what's up? You look positively strange!"

In a moment Alison had forgotten her resolution. In a whisper it all came out.

Maddy listened, astonished. "A ghost? You're joking."

But Alison corrected her. "She's not a ghost. At least I don't think of her like that."

Maddy snorted. "So where's this weirdo come from?"

"I told you. I pulled her out of the water."

"She was swimming? A swimming ghost? That's a good one."

"She's not a *she*, she's called Alicia. Oh, it's hard to explain."

"Groans and rattles chains does she?"

"Don't be daft. Of course she doesn't." Alison struggled to sort out her thoughts. "If she *is* a ghost she's not creepy. Not how you'd expect.

At least not to me. And if you're going to make fun of her then I don't want to talk about it."

Maddy realised that Alison was serious. Perhaps something *was* going on.

"Okay. So when can I come and see her?"

Alison shook her head.

"Oh, come on," urged Maddy.

She seemed to think it was all settled. "I can't come tonight 'cos it's my violin lesson, but tomorrow night's all right."

Alison hesitated. "Best wait till Monday."

"Monday? But it's only Tuesday now!"

"It's better Dado doesn't see you."

"What about the weekend?"

"Dado will still be around."

"Doesn't the old witch ever go out? Okay, Monday then."

Alison was beginning to wonder if she had been wise in telling Maddy anything.

"We might not even see her."

Maddy's expression changed. "Tell you what, I'll bring my camera. What a scoop, a picture of a ghost girl! Father will love it."

Maddy's father, Eddie Vinson, was a reporter on the *Newtown Gazette*. He had given Maddy an old camera, hoping she would become a press photographer.

Alison was alarmed. "You mustn't take her picture! It's a secret. I'm only letting you see her."

Maddy screwed up her face. "You're kidding. Once the *Gazette* gets it you'll be famous. Me too!"

Alison wished she had kept her mouth shut. "Look, I don't really know Alicia all that well."

Maddy's eyes narrowed. "So what are you saying, it's a joke?"

"Of course it's not!" Alison's voice rose. "She took hold of my hand. She's *real*, but we've got to keep it secret. And you mustn't bring a camera."

"Brilliant," said Maddy sarcastically. "It doesn't sound as if I'll need one."

Alison clenched her fists. Telling Maddy had definitely been a mistake. She caught Maddy's annoyed expression. "If I let you come you've got to be quiet and not rush up to her."

Maddy decided to agree. "All right, no camera, but it had better be good."

"Swear?"

"I just did, didn't I? I'll come on my bike after school."

"Not till Monday," insisted Alison.

The next few days were a misery. Alison spent every spare moment keeping watch for Alicia, but the girl did not appear. Perhaps she never would. Alison told Maddy this at school on Monday.

"I'm still coming," said Maddy, convinced now that something strange was going on.

Late in the afternoon Alison arrived home on the bus, and ten minutes later an excited Maddy pedalled up on her bike.

"We have to keep quiet," warned Alison.

They moved to the edge of the pond and Alison looked down into the water. There was no sign of the girl. A further careful look confirmed it.

"Sorry – she's not here."

Maddy frowned, shifting her camera under her blouse. "Perhaps she's hiding in the house?"

"She doesn't hide," said Alison crossly. "Not in the way you mean." She pointed at the boulder.

"The first time she was just here, but she could be anywhere."

And then she stood rigid.

"Shisssh! *There she is.*"

A slender figure was watching them from the other side of the pond. She was standing alongside the giant ash.

Quickly Maddy felt for the camera. "Where? Where is she? I can't see her."

"By the ash. On the left."

"The left?"

"To the left of the ash."

Maddy stared blankly at the tree.

"Can't you see her? She's as plain as anything."

Maddy could see no one. "You're kidding."

"I'm not!"

The girl was looking straight at them.

Maddy peered at the tree again and gave Alison a strange look. "You're nuts. There's no one there. *No one.*"

Alison was baffled. She could see Alicia clearly. A thought struck her: perhaps she was the only one who could see the girl and Maddy simply couldn't.

"If you think you're being funny, well you're not," snapped Maddy.

Without letting on to Alison, Maddy had already told the other girls in their class she was going to photograph a ghost. Acting quickly, she stepped back, pulled out her camera and snapped a picture of Alison from behind with the ash in the distance. She would show it round in school. *Alison and her invisible ghost!* It would be a laugh at least.

As Alison moved towards the tree the girl began to fade and disappear.

She did her best to explain: "It must be only me who can see her."

"Hah. That's a good one!"

"But it's true. I did," insisted Alison. "I do! She was here. As plain as day."

"And now she's run off, I suppose?"

"Yes. *No!* She just faded away as we got here."

Maddy screwed up her face. "I'll tell you what, you've a problem. It's mental!"

"I'm sorry. I did warn you."

Maddy snorted, grabbed her bike and rode away angrily. It would have made a brilliant story.

6 – THE SUN AND THE MOON

Aunt Dado produced a brown paper parcel and placed it on the kitchen dresser. "Finish your homework and after that I have a present for you, for your birthday."

The woman caught Alison's look of astonishment.

"*After* your homework," insisted Dado with a wan smile.

Never before had Dado given Alison a present. They had more or less got over their clash, but even so a present was unexpected. Her birthday had been weeks ago.

Alison struggled with her homework – maths again. The kitchen clock was striking eight before she had finished. Relieved, she put everything away, and only now opened the parcel. To her dismay, and then horror, a long red knitted woollen dress fell out.

Dado nodded. "Take it to your room and try it on. I found it on Oxfam's special rail."

Upstairs Alison fought to get into the thing. The dress was stretchy. It was like a tube, almost to her ankles. Her knees bulged into the knitting. She hated it.

"That is very sensible," said Dado, approvingly, as Alison came down the stairs trying not to trip. "You'll be able to wear it on special occasions."

Alison turned away and hid her dismay. At the same time she knew she was being unfair; it *was* a birthday present.

She crossed her fingers. "Thank you Aunt D, it's really lovely," she lied.

She went upstairs and changed back into jeans.

*

Another frustrating day at school. Alison was desperate to get home because Dado was going to be out.

Half past four came at last and Alison tumbled out of the bus and hurried down the track. She looked at the pond but saw no one. She went round to the back of the building. Again, no one.

When she was least expecting it she saw the girl standing in the field on the far side of the pond.

Please don't disappear, Alison whispered.

She climbed through the hedge and paused uncertainly, at a loss for words.

An age seemed to pass.

"Hello," she said shyly.

Alicia didn't turn. "You have been looking for me," she said. For the first time the girl's voice was clear and low. "I have watched you."

She looked drawn and fragile, and Alison felt a sudden urge to try to reassure this strange friend, for she was beginning to regard her as a friend. She drew near and sank to the ground, squatting cross-legged.

"Please, won't you stay and talk?"

She said it quietly, not daring to hope. To her delight, Alicia slowly sank down beside her.

Alison realised they could not have looked more different: Alicia white-faced, almost chalky and solemn, with a certain inner stillness. And herself, wild hair, constantly on the move, longing to know this strange girl better.

Alicia stared. "You have silver in your ears."

"They are ear-rings."

Alicia looked down.

"Your feet are big," she said.

Alison stayed silent. Alicia's bare feet were noticeably small. Alison decided that the girl was pretty but her clothes were drab and did not suit her. She wondered if she could give her something to cheer her up. Maybe a T-shirt. A cheerful yellow one

But no. Somehow, no.

A second thought came, a much better one… if only she could resolve to part with it.

Alicia's forlorn expression decided the matter.

Holding her breath, Alison reached behind her neck and lifted off her amber necklace. She leaned forward.

Don't, don't, please don't disappear.

She looped the necklace over Alicia's head so that it hung down onto her dress. It was the most precious thing Alison owned. She knew that her mother would have understood.

The amber caught the light.

"It's for you: it's a present."

A flicker of light crossed the girl's face.

"Now we are friends," smiled Alison.

Alicia touched the necklace with her delicate fingers; Alison could tell that the girl had never seen anything like it before.

"It is beautiful," said Alicia. "Yet you know I cannot take it."

"Please," said Alison, simply. "You can. It looks perfect on you."

Light shone through the leaves of the ash and dappled the water as Alicia fingered the tiny pieces of amber. For a moment the girl's face shone softly as if with an inner glow.

She looked steadily into Alison's eyes. It was a magical moment. "We are like the sun and the moon," she said softly. "We are like two sisters."

Alison's mind raced. *Sisters*. It was a wonderful thought. Perhaps they *were*.

A change seemed to come over Alicia. She sat up a shade straighter, looking sombre.

"There is something I have to tell," she said.

Her voice was suddenly very serious.

Alison stared, not understanding.

"I was with my little brother... we were high up in the ash. Up there."

The tree overlooked the water. Alison remembered the last time she had climbed up into its branches; it had been when her mother and father had died and she had desperately wanted to be alone and hide.

"It was me," said Alicia. "It was me who caused him to disappear. We had a fight."

The confession took Alison by surprise.

"He was only four…"

The words came out in a rush. The boy and girl had been wrestling in the forked branches, arguing, until it had all gone wrong. In a wild moment Alison's elbow had caught him in the face. She grabbed at him too late and both had fallen. He had struck the ground as she tumbled into the water.

Alicia spoke softly, her eyes troubled. "I could see him but I couldn't get to the bank. He seemed to shimmer and then he vanished. I tried so hard to get out but I felt trapped. The water wrapped around me and has held me a prisoner ever since. It has never let me go."

Trapped?

"But I pulled you out…"

Alicia looked down at the necklace. "Many have stopped by the water but you are the first to see me. You are the first person who knew I was here."

Alison was surprised. "Lots must have seen you."

"No one. Not ever."

It was an eerie thought. It made Alicia appear even lonelier.

"Your brother... you haven't told me his name."

"He will be near the house, somewhere near, I know it."

"Near? How do you mean?"

"He will be watching."

A shiver slid through Alison.

The girl noticed. "You must not be afraid. It is the old way. Sometimes those who have gone hide and keep watch on their loved ones. They guard and look after those who are here."

Alison had never heard of such a thing.

Alicia said: "Some nights I see shapes move on the bank with lanterns, and there are voices. I have *so* wanted to find him."

She paused. "He is called Peter. Little Peter. And now I am free I can start looking."

Impulsively Alison put a hand on the girl's arm. "We can look for him together," she said softly. "If you will let me."

Alicia's forlorn expression disappeared. For a moment she almost smiled. "Of course."

She pointed to the other side of the pond. "That's where we must start. At the voices. We must listen carefully."

"Listen?"

"Everything has its own special sound... I will know when I hear him."

Alison didn't think listening would do any good, but she said nothing.

They set off together, walking slowly. Alison was excited: she was having a real adventure. Supposing they found something creepy!

But the search did not go well. Several times Alicia paused for long spells, standing almost like a statue, unspeaking – once alongside a tree, and then again out in the open where a barn had stood. Each time they moved on until they reached a grassy patch.

Alicia looked troubled. "So many things have changed. There were cobbles here... this used to be a cart track."

Alison stared at the ground. To her it had always been a grassy path.

Alicia was downcast again. "I must think. We've looked enough for now."

"Another time?"

"Yes. I know he is here. "He *must* be."

Alicia began to fade.

"Oh, don't go!"

But in a moment she had disappeared and Alison felt more alone than ever.

7 – AUNT BETTY

A battered yellow Volvo car juddered to a halt at the back door of the farmhouse. There was a pause, then a cheerful dumpy, little figure in a woolly overcoat emerged from the driving seat. It was Betty, Alison's other aunt.

"But Alison's at school," said a puzzled Dado, putting away a packet of liquorish allsorts. *Why on earth was Betty here?*

"I know, dear, I know…"

Betty smiled as she sat herself down at the kitchen table. "I just wanted to find out how she is doing… I thought I'd come and have a nice cup of tea with you and see if she needs anything."

Checking up on me, you mean, thought Dado.

"How kind of you to come," she told Betty. "In fact she does need new shoes, but she's fine. I'm only surprised you asked."

"And the house?" said Betty, making sure she sounded casual. "Not yet settled?"

Dado made the tea. *So that was it! Betty wants to know what is going to happen about the house.*

"Nothing yet," Dado acknowledged. "I'm waiting for the solicitor to write. And if I may say so Betty, it really does not concern you. I was the one who agreed to look after Alison."

"Heavens, of course you did, dear!"

Betty stirred lots of sugar into her tea. She just hoped Alison was happy; she knew Dado could be a bit severe at times.

She opened her handbag and put two crisp £20 notes on the table. "Give her these, will you? I thought a little extra pocket money would cheer her up."

After Betty left, Dado decided that half of the money would be of more use in her own savings account. She was careful about money; she was aware she had plenty but there was no need to be reckless. The remaining £20 she folded into the cashbox to put towards Alison's new shoes. Betty had always been wasteful with money.

8 – INVITATION

Alison was excited. All thought of Alicia was temporarily forgotten: an important-looking letter had arrived for her at Cobbles Farm. The address on the front was handwritten but the sender's name had been printed on the back of the envelope in small letters.

"What's that you've got?" asked Dado.

They were at the breakfast table. Alison read out the sender's name: "Wilkinson & Drone, Solicitors, Newtown."

"A solicitor? Let me see."

Dado took it off her.

"How ridiculous – this should have been sent to me."

"But it's got my name!" said Alison.

Dado looked doubtful, as if she were going to open the letter herself.

"It's been sent to me!" insisted Alison. Whatever was her aunt doing?

Reluctantly Dado handed it back.

"Just make sure it really is for you."

Alison tore it open. The letter was short. It was from a Mr J L Wilkinson. It asked her to phone his office to arrange an appointment to discuss her parents' will. Her aunt, Miss D Fletcher, who would receive a separate letter, was to come with her.

*

There was no phone at Cobbles Farm but it did not stop Dado. "Give that to me and I'll phone tomorrow when I go into town."

Alison kept tight hold. "No thank you, Aunt D, I can do it. There's a phone box outside the school."

Dado stared, not enjoying being contradicted. "Make sure you do. I have a definite feeling this is to do with me. It's about who owns the place."

Alison pretended she hadn't heard, but she was shocked. Wasn't the farm hers? Of course, it wasn't really a farm any more; it was just a private house now. Even so, it wasn't Dado's. It *couldn't* be.

She remembered the day her father had converted the upstairs box room into her own private den. He had put up lots of bookshelves and bought her a second-hand desk, which she had painted white. It was lovely, with a set of drawers and a swivel stool.

"This will always be your secret den," he had told her.

Not any more. Dado had made the den into an ironing room where the washing could be sorted. To Alison's dismay, her desk was stored down in the cellar and the den was no longer a den. Despite that, she knew that the house was supposed to be hers and not Dado's. She *knew* it was.

9 – PHOTO MYSTERY

In a small terrace house at the top end of Newtown, Maddy was hard at work. She plugged a red light bulb into the pantry socket. It was still only six in the morning but already she was dressed and had removed the film from her camera. She pushed a towel into a window and blocked out the daylight, turning the room into a photographic studio.

Her camera was old, not smart like the digis her pals flashed around, but her dad had insisted it was still good and when used carefully would take good photographs.

In the next half-hour Maddy developed the film. There were twenty-four shots.

Though the tiny negative of Alison was still a bit damp, she put it into the enlarger and let the light shine through it onto a sheet of printing paper. It took seconds to expose, then she dropped the sheet into the dish of developer liquid. A ghost? Huh, she would show Alison Benson. That one was getting too hoity-toity!

As the picture began to appear, Maddy recognised Alison who was standing facing the forked ash. Then she stared again more carefully: there seemed to be something else in the picture.

There were *two* figures… a girl was standing by the tree!

Maddy gaped. Besides Alison and herself, there had been no one else there. There *hadn't*! She *knew* there hadn't.

Already the picture was disappearing. Yuk! She hadn't put it in the fixing chemical to stop it fading!

She did another print. Using a magnifying glass, she saw that the second girl was about the same height as Alison but had short dark hair.

A bigger print was needed.

Excited, she juggled with the enlarger lens and focussed on the unknown girl.

The result was awful – a large hazy picture of the girl's face. This time she let the print lie longer in the chemical fixer. It should have stopped the picture fading away, but it didn't. To her surprise the picture began to vanish.

Quickly she printed a new copy, and again the mystery girl's outline was there. But for some reason it turned into a white patch, a silhouette.

Maddy kept trying, but it became worse: more and more detail was disappearing. Eventually there was only a white space where the girl had been standing. Baffled, she took the negative out of the enlarger and was astonished to find that the little black and white negative itself had changed. The girl had vanished, only her silhouette was there, plain to see.

It *couldn't* be a ghost! It simply couldn't.

She would show it to Alison. She would show her on Monday.

*

Maddy caught up with Alison at school break and waved a print.

"A photo?" said Alison. "You told me you wouldn't!" She grabbed it off her. "Let me see!"

"Hey, don't crumple it."

Alison was dismayed. Her first thought was to pretend the photograph was a fake, but she knew it wasn't. The white silhouette clearly was Alicia.

"You had no right to take it. What are you going to do with it?"

Maddy shrugged. "Nothing," she lied. "But I want to try again to see her."

"Well you can't," said Alison. "Aunt Dado will get to know if people start coming round."

"Then I'll send her this picture," snapped Maddy, "Then she'll really get to know!"

She marched off.

An uneasy afternoon followed. As lessons ended, Alison caught sight of Maddy and two other girls in a huddle. Whatever happened, Alison was determined not to reveal anything else. She no longer trusted Maddy.

10 – A STRANGE WILL

Dado drove Alison into Newtown to meet the solicitor, Mr Wilkinson. He was young looking and quiet-mannered, with a rather lean, suntanned face. He smiled kindly as Alison and her aunt took seats in his office.

"I have never before come across such an unusual will," he confessed straight away. "It presents us immediately with a problem."

He produced a buff-coloured envelope.

Alison sat forward excitedly. She could see her name was written on it and her heart missed a beat. It was in her father's handwriting.

"My late partner Mr Drone handled this matter some years ago. It is one of the most unusual sets of instructions I have ever dealt with."

"So what's wrong with it, then?" asked Dado.

"I am sorry to say it is not legal."

Dado's face screwed up. "Not legal? That's nonsense!"

The man shook his head. "The will is very old-fashioned. Wills are not written like this today. I'm afraid we must have a modern will to prove who owns the farm."

He held out the envelope. "Perhaps Miss Alison would care to have a look?"

Feeling important, Alison opened the envelope. A ragged slip of paper tumbled out.

"Oh, it's torn."

Mr Wilkinson smiled. "No, I don't think so. But we do have a problem – and a mystery."

The ragged strip was covered in writing.

"Is it a will or isn't it?" demanded Dado crossly. "Does it say who owns the house, or doesn't it?"

She avoided Alison's angry glare.

Mr Wilkinson replied. "Yes – that is to say, it used to."

He turned to Alison. "The will was written on a single sheet of paper. Then the page was cut, or more likely torn into three pieces. This is one of them."

Dado snorted in disgust. "And what good is that?"

The solicitor smiled. "It's an old way of protecting documents. It fits together like a three-piece jigsaw."

He picked up the ragged strip and showed Alison.

"The pieces were shared out to three different people; each person takes care of his or her own piece."

His eyes shone. "Only when all three are put together can the will be read properly... but Miss Fletcher, I think you know this already. I believe my late partner Mr Drone sent you one of the pieces to take care of?"

Alison stared at Dado. Her aunt had never mentioned this.

"I expect you have already shown it to Miss Alison?"

Dado looked annoyed. She opened her bag and took out a second buff envelope.

"I was keeping it safe until it was needed."

Her face had turned pink.

"Of course," smiled Mr Wilkinson. "Now we can join up two of the pieces."

Dado laid Alison's zigzag strip on the desk. It was the left-hand side of a page and was covered in handwriting.

The other zigzag piece was the right-hand side. Carefully Mr Wilkinson fitted the two pieces together. "Good. Now only the bottom of the page is missing. However, I shall read out the important parts to you from these two pieces.

THE WILL AND TESTAMENT
OF
ANDREW AND MARY BENSON
Until she is twenty-one,
Alison Benson,
their daughter
at the property Cobbles Farm
shall be occupied by her
under the GUIDANCE of a
Guardian D Fletcher,
of Newtown.
To D Fletcher we entrust
a Third of this Will document
to her care
With the sum of £5,000
while so caring
She will also Receive an Allowance
to be Determined by
J L Wilkinson and Drone

the aforesaid
solicitors for as long as she takes
Good Care of
The before mentioned
Alison Benson.

"So, is that everything?" asked Dado sharply.

For the first time Mr Wilkinson frowned. "No, no." He glanced at Dado, surprised by her manner. "Somewhere there will be the third part of the will. The piece that goes across the bottom of the page."

He paused and looked at Alison. "I find myself wondering if the other aunt has it – that is to say, Miss Betty… er, Miss Delia Fletcher?"

Dado looked scornful. "Nonsense, Betty's far too scatty to be trusted with a will. Surely a complete copy must have been left here in your office? I cannot believe there isn't one."

Mr Wilkinson shook his head. "That is the mystery. Miss Alison's part was waiting here, to be read now that she's twelve. And here we have yours. I expect the missing piece will be in some drawer or cupboard at the farm."

"It is no longer a farm," said Dado snappily. "It is now a private house."

Mr Wilkinson's voice did not change. "Wherever the third piece is, I sincerely hope a modern will is with it. We do need it."

Dado took the two pieces from Alison and read them for herself. "It seems clear enough. It says a third of the place comes to me."

Mr Wilkinson held up a hand. "No, it says a third of the will is for you to look after. That means one piece of the document is for you to take care of; it does not mean you own a third of the farm."

Dado spluttered. "What nonsense!"

"Unless we can find a modern will," said Mr Wilkinson, "we can do no more. Our hands are tied."

Dado reached forward. "Then I'll take care of these."

But Mr Wilkinson stopped her. "No. The matter is not yet settled. For now I must keep the originals safe here. However, I will send both of you photo copies."

He collected up the two ragged strips.

Dado said no more and Alison could see she was angry.

They drove home at a frightening speed. Alison held fast onto the seat and pretended Alicia was with her and they were having a secret conversation.

Dado's going dotty. The house isn't hers.

Of course it isn't.

But she says it is.

She's lying. She just wants to steal it.

How can she?

She's horrible about money. I wish she would go.

Alison bit at her lip. She was very glad Mr Wilkinson was on her side.

11 – DESPERATE SEARCH

A day passed. Alison felt at a loss. School, school, school, and tons of homework. She arrived home knowing a long, weary evening lay ahead.

Something went bump in the living room; she dumped her school bag on the kitchen table and hurried through. Dado was tipping up a drawer and emptying out the contents.

"Aunt D, what is it?"

Papers and books were strewn on the carpet. Dado gave her a strange look. "What do you think? I'm looking for the stupid will."

She tipped up the drawer and got a last piece of paper out. "Don't just stand there, child; go and set the table!"

Alison stomped out, slamming the door. Always giving orders!

Dado had searched the house. The rooms were littered with letters, old envelopes, billheads, newspapers and photographs. Worse, Alison was shocked to find that a line of her father's paintings had been taken down and were standing on the floor, propped against a wall.

She tried to hang them up again but the nails had gone. She bit back her tears. Her aunt was a spiteful old witch.

Worse came next day.

After school she hurried down the track, wishing she could tell someone what was happening. If only Aunt Betty didn't live so far away in town. She at least would have listened.

She pushed into the kitchen and was startled by the sound of hammering. It was coming from upstairs. Broken plaster spilled down the staircase, where a shallow hole gaped in the wall to reveal bare stonework. She hurried up to her aunt's room.

Dado was pounding a wall with a hammer and chisel. She was in overalls and had tied a scarf round her head. Alison gaped. Dust filled the place and two more holes showed in the stonework where the plaster had been hacked away.

"Aunt D…"

Dado's face was covered in sweat. She shot Alison a look of annoyance. "There's no will in any of the cupboards or drawers. But there's *got* to be a hiding place somewhere. A secret cupboard. The solicitor said as much. Now leave me alone!"

The solicitor said no such thing, thought Alison. She lingered as Dado hammered at the plaster.

The woman turned, her face crimson. "*Go away!*" she shouted.

Alison fled downstairs. Her aunt was going potty!

12 – HALF-CLOSED EYES

The hammering continued to echo throughout the house. As there was nothing else to eat, Alison made herself beans on toast. She was tempted to ignore her homework but knew it would mean trouble in the morning so she ate the beans and set about writing a long piece about the causes of the French Revolution. Because it worked out well and she finished it quickly, she did a geography question on the effects of locust plagues in Africa.

She was busily writing when Dado came down. Her aunt didn't speak; she made a cheese sandwich and a cup of instant coffee and went back upstairs, her face tightly drawn. It was growing late, but the hammering started again.

Alison had had enough. Annoyed, she hurried out to the ash tree and sank down behind its trunk so that she was out of sight. Cobbles Farm no longer felt like the happy place it used to be. For the first time, she felt afraid without knowing what she was afraid of.

"You are troubled again," said a low voice.

Alison gasped. Alicia's sudden appearances were always a shock.

"Ow, I wish you wouldn't."

The girl's face shone faintly.

Distant hammering sounded.

Alison said: "She's knocking the walls to bits. She's trying to find a will."

"She is angry," said Alicia. "I think something is going to happen."

She did not explain what.

Alison could hear that Alicia was tired.

"Are you still searching?"

"Everywhere. There seems nowhere else to look."

The pale light of the moon was starting to filter through the trees.

Alison longed to know Alicia better, but there never seemed to be any time. "Let's look tomorrow," she suggested. "I'll help you search."

They sank down by the big boulder where it dipped into the water, two figures in the half-light.

"I see you are sad," said Alicia.

"Not always."

"You miss your parents."

"Yes."

"They used to stand here by the water," said Alicia. "The two of them."

Alison smiled. She knew it was true. She said: "Dad painted every day, lovely pictures, and people would come and buy them. Mum painted too, to go into books.

"I'd sit in Dad's studio up in the barn and keep quiet so as not to bother him. In the summer he'd open the upper door and the swallows would swoop over us in the rafters as he painted. They never collided, though you'd think they would. And after the swallows, when it was dark, the bats flew in, ever so quickly, and they were just as clever and never hit into anything, and Dad still went on painting, using a lamp, even with them flying around.

"He was very funny. Some mornings we'd go for walks to look for ideas. He'd stop suddenly in the road and draw in his notebook.

"His squiggles looked really daft. One was really wild. I asked him what it was and he said, 'I am drawing light'. I asked how was that possible, and I've never forgotten his answer: 'If you are a true artist you can draw anything.'

"His notebooks were full of tiny pictures. Birds and trees, chimney pots – lovely things. He drew them in pencil, so everything was in black or grey. But he could remember the colours – even a year later. When he wanted to paint them he looked in his notebooks at the shapes and remembered each colour perfectly."

"How did he do that?"

"He said the colours were all waiting in his head. And they were. Sometimes I could do the same, remember colours I mean. I loved painting and wanted to be an artist.

"Mum painted flowers for flower catalogues. And insects. Beetles and dragonflies and earwigs, oh lots of earwigs! She was good and wanted me to draw them too, and I drew and drew and did lots, but never earwigs.

"We were so happy…"

She broke off, remembering how it had all changed. Now there were two aunts in her life: Dado and Betty. Without knowing why, she loved dumpy Aunt Betty more than anyone, yet it was Dado with her long grey hair who had taken over the house and had decided to look after her.

Alicia said: "Where are your drawings?"

"I dug a hole."

"A hole?"

"I buried them down in the ground."

Alicia was surprised. "Didn't you want to be an artist?"

Alison shook her head. With her mother and father gone she had changed. She felt alone.

"I stopped."

She fell silent, thinking how strange everything had become. She looked at Alicia and smiled. The two girls sat without speaking for a while.

Then Alison said: "You *are* a ghost, aren't you? I mean, a real one? But I'm not scared. Not even a bit. And you lived here, didn't you, at the farm... with your mum and your dad and your brother. Long before me. I know you did."

Alicia skimmed a stone onto the pond. It skittered across the moonlit water, creating silver circles before sinking. "We came when it was built," she said softly.

Alison was surprised. All that time ago? The house was built in 1907 – she had seen the date carved into a stone over the front doorway.

Alicia seemed unaware of her surprise.

"Father was a farm worker."

She threw another stone and they counted as it bounced four times before it sank.

"Do you know what a scythe is?"

"Of course," said Alison. She'd seen one at the Watson's farm down the road – a sharp metal blade on the end of a long pole. "It's for cutting grass."

"For hay, especially…" Alicia's voice held a touch of pride. "Father was strong. He could cut hay better than anyone. Every time he swung his scythe he cut it just right. It's very hard to do. He said it must fall to the land in perfect lengths, and when he cut it, it did.

"Mother was nothing like him. He was tall and she was small. She cooked and made us laugh. She spent hours whitewashing the house; climbing ladders to do the high bits."

"My house? Here, where I live?" said Alison.

She stared across at the front of the building, pale and ghostly in the moonlight. It was no longer whitewashed, just weathered stone. Yet it fitted the land perfectly.

"Yes." Alicia paused. "I love it." Her voice faltered.

Of course, Cobbles had been Alicia's home too. Alison realised that she was still missing it. "I'm sorry…" And then: "I wish you could live here again, I mean with me, in my home… *your* home, where you lived. Together."

Like two sisters.

She knew it was impossible. A ghost sister.

"Few would be happy if I did," said Alicia. She went on: "Little Peter and I had a secret game. When the moon shone, just like now, we'd walk on the grass and search for magic lights. We'd creep out in the middle of the night and no one would know we were not in bed."

Seeing Alison didn't understand she stood up. "I'll show you. But without those. They will hear you."

"Who will?"

Alicia only pointed.

Alison pulled off her shoes and socks and together the girls went out into the field beyond the pond. The grass was damp and they walked bare-footed on the cool carpet, talking softly.

"Now we must search."

Alison thrilled as Alicia slipped a hand into hers.

A speck of light shone in the grass. Then, further away, another speck appeared, green and bright; and moments later they saw two more. Alison realised excitedly that they were glow-worms.

"Whoever finds ten first is the winner!" said Alicia.

"Ten? We'll never!"

They began to pick them up, one by one, until the tiny green lights shone in their cupped hands. Alicia won and they both laughed. It was the first time Alison had heard her laugh.

Alicia said: "Little Peter called them magic lights but you can see they are beetles. I always won. He could only count to six!" She paused, then added: "Tomorrow I must find him. I *must*."

They dropped the glow-worms back into the grass.

The sky was starry now. A million bright specks. *A million glow-worms*, Alison told herself.

"Let's see if the world is still turning," said Alicia.

"But it is!" said Alison, surprised.

"Yes, but we must make sure. It would be terrible if it had stopped. We must watch a special star."

The sky was full of constellations. Some were easy to find. Alison knew which one was the Plough because it looked like a saucepan; and that the giant one shaped like a W was Cassiopeia, though she could hardly pronounce the word.

Alicia pointed to a star low down in the sky. "That's the one we must watch. Not everyone knows how to play this game."

It shone brighter than all the others. Alison thought it must be Venus but she couldn't remember. It glittered through the branches of the trees.

Alicia said: "If we keep looking at it we will see the world move."

"How?"

"Just watch."

Alison stared at the star. Gradually it edged across the sky until it reached the silhouette of a tree. Then it moved behind the blackness of a branch and its light was blotted out.

Alicia said: "You must not think the star is moving. It is the world that is moving, the world is turning with the tree joined on to it."

Alison stayed silent. Seconds passed and slowly a glimmer of light began to appear from behind the branch. Little by little the star emerged again.

"The branch moved!" said Alicia. "The branch and us – the whole world – because we are all joined to it. And the tree hid the star as we turned. Now we know the world is turning."

Alison had never thought about it before. Of course she knew the world was turning all the time, but she had always let herself think it was the stars that were moving. Well, perhaps they were, only far away. It was all a bit tricky.

Alicia said: "Peter liked magic lights best."

Alison said nothing. She was simply too happy to speak.

"I'll race you," said Alicia.

Giddily they ran up and down the field and as they chased one another they yelled and laughed, their arms spread out like wings. They were flying! They were sisters. They flew in the moonlight.

13 – CLASSROOM REVENGE

Maddy was determined to get her own back on Alison. The chair at her desk had become wobbly and Maddy used it as an excuse to cross from her place in the middle of the classroom to take the seat against the wall behind Alison.

Miss Marsden, the teacher, blinked shortsightedly through her heavy glasses and did not seem to notice her move. It was English Lit. She told the class to read a chapter from *Charlotte's Web* and write a summary in fifty words. This pleased Alison. It was her favourite story.

Maddy started to fiddle about. She was crafty about it. She rustled some papers as if she had lost something; then she searched inside the desk, tutting softly. She scratched herself noisily on a leg. She dropped a pencil. She made an irritating noise or movement every time Miss Marsden's attention was elsewhere.

Alison soon realised that Maddy was doing it deliberately. It was annoying, but she pretended not to notice and went on writing the summary.

At twelve o'clock the buzzer sounded for lunch. Maddy got up slowly as the classroom emptied and for once she held back and fussed about putting her books away.

Then she lifted the lid of Alison's desk.

＊

A hot netball session ensued. Alison loved every minute and scored twice. Netball was one of her favourite games. As it was, she had just time to shower and eat her sandwiches, and then get back to the classroom.

Maths again! Alison groaned. The sharp-faced Mrs Sheldon, the math's teacher, checked the register and made sure everyone was there before turning to chalk a first problem on the blackboard.

Alison reached into her desk for her math's book, but it was as far as she got. The book looked different. Puzzled, she touched it and found it was covered in glue. And not just her math's book; everything in the desk was sticky, the pens and pencils, her notebooks – even the copy of *Charlotte's Web*!

She guessed at once who was to blame. She turned and stared behind her. Maddy had her head down and was hard at work writing.

Alison glared angrily. It was not often she felt antagonistic, but this time Maddy had gone too far. Well, two could play at that game!

She undid her penknife, wiped it on her hanky. Waiting for the right moment, she moved across to Maddy's desk in the middle of the room. For a moment she pretended to examine the uneven chair, then pressing hard, she carved a deep letter X on the desktop.

Had anyone noticed? It seemed that no one had, but perhaps Maddy had.

Yes, she had! She was staring at Alison open-mouthed.

*

"I tell you, I saw her do it!" yelled Maddy.

Charlotte and Emma listened as she went through the whole thing yet again. Both had looked at the scratch and dutifully agreed it was awful.

Emma said: "Are you going to scratch *her* desk and get your own back?"

"And get caught? No. I told you, no one saw her do it except me. Not even Mrs Sheldon. She scratched it really hard."

"Mrs Sheldon?"

"No, *stupid*. Alison."

Charlotte and Emma looked uncomfortable. Maddy could be really unpleasant at times.

"Why didn't you tell Mrs Sheldon?" said Charlotte.

"Because I didn't, did I? I just told you, she wasn't even looking. Well, two can play at that game!"

Revenge was on Maddy's mind. "I'll tell you *exactly* what I'm going to do… and don't split on me or I'll thump you."

14 – SECRET SOUNDS

It was early morning and already there was the sound of hammering.

Alison and Alicia were by the big boulder.

Alicia said: "I think your aunt is being unkind."

Alison shrugged. Dado was not all bad but that did not mean she had to like her, not all the time anyway. "She goes out a lot to see friends. She's going tomorrow."

"Then tomorrow," said Alicia, "I must listen again for Peter. I *must* find him."

Alison hesitated, reluctant to say what she was thinking. "But it's so long ago. How can you hope to find him after all this time?"

It sounded impossible.

"If he is near I'll hear him."

She saw the puzzled look on Alison's face.

"You don't believe me…"

She looked at the ground and pointed at a patch of fallen leaves. "Quick, look under there! Something is hiding."

Alison stared.

"Go on! I can hear it."

Alison didn't know whether to believe her or not, but she scuffed at the leaves with a foot.

Something grey and furry raced for cover.

She stared, astonished. It had been a field mouse. "How did you know that was there?"

Alicia didn't answer; she pointed again. "Look at that stone. The flat one."

It was a piece of broken slate.

"Listen hard. *Really hard*. Something's moving."

Alison blinked.

"There's more than one."

Bending swiftly, Alicia lifted it up.

"See!"

Three tiny black beetles ran for cover.

Alison was startled. "But you can't have heard *them*! Not beetles. Not just like that. No one could!"

A flicker of a smile lit Alicia's face. "But I did. *I do*. I listen. The world is full of little sounds; things moving in secret. If other people listened hard enough they'd hear them, too. See, there's something else…"

She turned over a leaf. A tiny moth flew away.

"You couldn't hear that! Not a moth."

"I did. Its wings fluttered."

Despite her doubts, Alison was impressed. "How can you *hear* these things? I bet nobody else can."

Alicia said nothing for a moment. Then: "You could if I taught you."

Alison smiled disbelievingly.

"Yes, you could… I know it."

A moorhen splashed noisily among the irises, sending ripples across the pond.

"I shall teach you," said Alicia, suddenly decided. "But only if you really try. You must want it to happen, and you must not be scared."

"Scared?"

Alicia had a gleam in her eyes. "Sometimes I think I can hear the earth itself turning, deep deep down. A slow rumble. It can be scaring! But that's only at times. Mostly the sounds I hear are tiny."

A breeze stirred the surface of the pond and moved away through the trees. "Won't you try with me?" Alicia's voice grew softer. "Just try and forget everything… except to listen."

Alison did not speak, then because she felt embarrassed, and to please her friend as much as anything, she told herself she might as well try. She would pretend, anyway.

"Close your eyes…"

For what seemed an age – though it was hardly half a minute – Alison stood and listened, knowing that nothing would happen. Nothing *could*.

Nor did it. All she could hear was the wind in the trees.

Alicia, pale and intent, saw it hadn't worked. "Wait, there may be another way. Do as I do. Try touching the ground as you listen."

To show what she meant Alicia knelt and let her fingertips touch a grassy patch.

"Go on, like me."

Alison copied her. But it all seemed so silly!

Time passed. Blank empty moments and slowly she felt as if she were being drawn into an empty space. Because nothing was happening her shoulders relaxed and something began to walk noisily along beneath her left hand.

"Oh!"

She pulled away, startled. Yet nothing was there! But something *had* been, she had heard it!

Quickly Alicia put a finger to her lips.

The noise had stopped.

Alicia said: "I forgot to tell you... if you hear something moving don't speak, or it will stop. But you did hear something, didn't you? I can tell."

Alison, amazed, nodded.

"I knew you could do it. Shall we try again?"

The drumming of a car engine sounded.

Alicia stood up. "We'll try again later. It will be easier next time."

15 – FLYING VISIT

The car drew in at the back of the house and a cheerful dumpy figure in a woolly overcoat knocked at the kitchen door. Alison's face lit up. It was Aunt Betty.

"I've only got fifteen minutes, then I have to go," her aunt told her.

Alison rushed to put the kettle on.

Betty rummaged in her holdall, waved her passport, waved her purse, and then tugged out a small parcel. "A quick cuppa would be ace. On my way to France! A holiday! Yes, I've been a bit unwell – too many cream cakes – but I'm better. Passport's come just in time. And this…"

She smiled impishly and handed Alison a parcel.

"Got crushed. Hope it's your size. A blouse. A very late birthday present. I can get it changed if you don't like it." She grinned.

Alison tore open the wrapping. The blouse was perfect. Faint blue and white stripes. She loved it instantly. She looked at the passport.

"Aunt B, why do you call yourself Betty? I mean your real name is Delia."

Betty smiled. "I've always been called Betty. And Delia's a bit old fashioned, and it would be a bit funny changing things now. But whatever's going on?"

Betty stared at the kitchen floor and a heap of debris left by Dado's last attack on a wall. "Goodness me."

"Oh Aunt Betty, it's all going wrong."

Before she knew it Alison burst into tears and the whole thing came out: Dado's hunt for the lost piece of the will, how she was knocking things to bits as she searched for hidden cupboards. The endless hammering.

Betty listened, at first open-mouthed, and then in dismay as they went into each room and she saw the mess. She even looked into the pantry where the inner brick walls had been pounded and the shelves were littered with plaster.

"Whatever's got into her?" she said. "This is terrible! We can't have this."

"I keep trying to clear up," said Alison, but she gives me strange looks. I hate her!"

Betty was desperately sorry. "It's no use, I really can't stay any longer today. The plane. But I'll come and see you the moment I'm back from France. Two weeks. Now you must stop worrying – I'll sort her out."

She looked grim.

The farmhouse, eh? She always did go on about money and such, though she's got plenty.

She gave Alison a comforting hug.

"I'll be back, I promise. I'll put a stop to all this."

She had to go.

An hour later Dado arrived home and heard about Betty's visit.

"It's all right for some," was all she would say. By which Alison guessed that Dado disapproved of Betty.

16 – GHOST RIDERS

The three girls met in the garden shed at Maddy's. It was Saturday morning.

"Give me the vest," Maddy ordered.

Charlotte undid the parcel and was surprised.

"It looks new."

"It's not. Now give me the stuffing. Come on!" demanded Maddy.

Emma had brought a plastic carrier bag. She pulled out a tangle of old tights.

"They're full of holes," she said, apologetically.

Maddy snorted. "That doesn't matter. She's not going to wear them."

Charlotte still looked bothered about the vest. She knew she would have used an old one had it been up to her.

Maddy knotted the shoulder straps of the vest, then Emma pushed the worn-out tights in at the open end until it looked about the size of a head.

"Pass me the pole."

Charlotte laid a brush handle on a bench and they nailed a short piece of wood across it near the top to make the shoulders. Maddy forced the stuffed head onto the top of the pole and tied it with a piece of baler twine.

"Now open the sheet."

Charlotte and Emma exchanged glances. The sheet had bold orange and white stripes and had been freshly laundered. They knew Maddy had got it out of her mother's airing cupboard.

Maddy shook the sheet open and cut a slot in the middle with a pair of scissors. She forced the head through the hole. The ghost now had a flowing robe.

"It would be better if it was a white one, but it will do."

She prized open a tin of black paint. Because Charlotte had the steadiest hand, Maddy got her to paint two long, haunting eyes on the ghost's face. Then they propped it against the workbench to have a proper look.

Emma said: "It doesn't look all that scary. It just looks funny."

"When it's dark it will scare her all right," promised Maddy. "Now, get here at eight o'clock."

"What if we don't see her? What if she stays in?"

"Then we'll make her come out. You can moan outside her window, that'll make her come out."

Emma pouted. "I don't want to moan. Not by myself."

"Then we'll *all* moan."

"But it might not be dark and she'll be able to tell it's us!"

"Stop worrying. We'll wait till it's really dark. But make sure you've got your bike lights so we can light up the ghost."

"I might not be able to come," said Emma.

"Then we'll go without you and you'll miss all the fun," said Maddy, annoyed at Emma's lack of courage.

They hid the ghost behind the shed door. Alison was in for a nasty surprise.

*

Saturday had never seemed to drag before. It was windy, and spots of rain in the early afternoon had bothered Maddy in case another deluge was coming. But the rain held off and by teatime she knew it was going to be all right. She loaded a new film into her camera and tested the flash.

Mr Vinson, in a crumpled grey suit and with a permanent frown, gulped down a mug of tea. He was rushing off to report an evening meeting.

"You're not taking photos out in this weather are you?" he demanded.

"It's something special," said Maddy.

"Then make sure no rain gets on the lens."

"Dad, I won't! I know what I'm doing!"

Giggling with excitement, the girls met again in the shed. It was almost eight o'clock and heavy clouds had turned the sky dark. Perfect weather for a good haunting.

"I hope you've oiled your bikes so they don't squeak," warned Maddy.

They hadn't.

She found the oilcan. Then she rolled up the ghost. The paint was still tacky and they tied it to her bike so its head stuck out at the back.

"The wind will help dry it. Now let's go."

The ghost riders set out for Cobbles.

The wind proved a nuisance. Twenty minutes of hard pedalling ensued before they arrived out of breath and glad to get off their bikes. They hid them at the roadside and set off up the track.

Suppressing nervous giggles, they sank into long grass near the pond.

"She's in," hissed Maddy.

Beyond the pond a light was shining in a downstairs window. Its light reflected in the water.

"Well, don't just lie there dozing! Help me sort it!"

Keeping low, Charlotte and Emma unravelled the ghost and spread it on the ground. Charlotte snapped twigs off a bush to clear a way so they could raise the pole easily when the moment came.

Maddy set her camera down on a stone where she could grab it.

All was ready.

"Lift the ghost up the moment I say," Maddy ordered Emma.

But Emma was beginning to wish she was safely back at home. "Couldn't you do the lifting? You're bigger than us, and it's heavy."

"Brilliant," sneered Maddy. "How can I take a photo if I'm holding the ghost? And one of you's got to shine the torch to light it up. It'll be no good if it's not lit up will it?"

"But what if she doesn't come out?" persisted Emma.

"If she doesn't come out then you can throw pebbles at the windows and make her. Now shut up."

17 – SHRIEKS IN THE DARK

Alison decided to experiment in secret. She stood in the dark alongside the garden gate, determined to concentrate and listen hard – but this time without Alicia. Perhaps it wouldn't work when she was by herself. She stood unmoving, prepared to wait. At first it was easy, though as the minutes passed and nothing happened she became frustrated. She put a hand on the gate to steady herself.

A faint clicking came from close by her right foot, but it stopped almost at once. She stiffened. Hardly daring to breathe, she clutched at the gate and closed her eyes, and this seemed to help. There! It happened again. Something was moving! But not only that: there were other noises. Lots! Slowly the ground around her seemed to be filling with other tiny sounds. Small movements, something spidery running, a faint jostling. She listened, not daring to move. The longer she stood the stronger the sounds became. Things coming and going.

Something whirled past in the blackness, briefly sensed, then gone – a bat, turning on the wind. Far away an owl hooted in the dark. But it was the tiny sounds in the ground below her feet that held her attention. She was longing to turn over stones and look, and was on the point of risking it when there was an interruption.

From the far side of the pond came a strange sighing of air, a soft disturbance, scarcely discernable. It took her a moment to realise what it was: she could hear whispering.

A moment later a shriek filled the night and she almost tripped in surprise.

She got to the water's edge as a ghostly figure shone on the far bank. It was Alicia! She was standing in the long grass alongside three terrified figures.

Momentarily they seemed to be frozen, then down at their feet something glinted, vanished, glinted again, and a shiny object tumbled down the bank and landed in the water. There was a wild rush of air.

The three girls ran for their lives, shrieking.

Alison waited tensely.

"No one will spy on you again," said a satisfied voice.

Alicia was at her side, still glowing eerily.

"What did you do?" gasped Alison.

Alicia shrugged her shoulders as the glow faded. "Nothing – I just appeared among them and stared. They didn't seem to enjoy that very much."

Alison almost laughed. "Maddy – that's the big one – that was her camera that fell into the water, wasn't it? She'd be trying to take a photograph."

Alicia didn't answer.

"She's always taking pictures," explained Alison. "Her father wants her to be a newspaper photographer."

"You like her?"

The question sounded almost abrupt.

"She's not exactly a friend. But how could she see you? Last time she couldn't."

"When I want, then she can."

Alicia's shining form was fading.

"Oh, wait!" cried Alison.

Maddeningly, Alicia vanished.

18 – MIRROR FRIGHT

Maddy kept well away next day at school. Alison smiled to herself. Maddy might be big and bossy but she no longer seemed all that brave.

Yet all was not well. The moment Alison arrived home, she sensed something was going to happen. Dado was tense and watchful.

Not until they had eaten did her aunt drop the bombshell. "I have been thinking about the will. I have decided I must let someone else look at the two parts. I'm not satisfied with the way Mr Wilkinson is handling matters."

She paused and fastened back her hair with a clip. "After a lot of consideration I've decided to sell the house."

She glanced sharply at Alison.

It took a moment for Alison to realise what her aunt was saying.

"But the farm is supposed to be mine!"

"No, no. I don't think the will says that. I think the solicitor has got it wrong."

Wrong? thought Alison angrily. *Only if it doesn't suit you, you old cow*!

Dado pressed on: "I've read both parts again. It seems all I have to do is provide you with a home until you are twenty-one. That doesn't have to mean here at Cobbles."

Alison grew wide-eyed. "It doesn't say that! You know it doesn't!"

"Well I think it does. It could mean another house elsewhere – in fact wherever I choose to live. And that is my intention. I'm going to build a bungalow and you will have a room all to yourself. Of course, I'll still look after you."

Alison was shocked. The thought of losing Cobbles filled her with dismay.

"But Mr Wilkinson said it's mine! I know he did!"

Ignoring her, Dado talked more briskly: "This house is expensive to run. I want to get rid of it quickly and get a good price. I'll go on looking for the proper will but meanwhile I'll arrange for us to live elsewhere while the bungalow is built."

"But Mr Wilkinson…"

Dado didn't seem to hear. "I'm going to sort it out on Monday with my own solicitor."

Alison was dumbfounded. The house wasn't Dado's! It couldn't be! Worse… if they moved she would no longer be able to see Alicia. "I'm going out," she declared, angrily.

"Out? But it's pouring down."

"I'll use the big umbrella."

"Don't be silly! You'll catch your death of cold. And I'm tired of having to tell you. Your mother and father would have been appalled at your behaviour."

Alison flared. "Mum and Dad were a lot nicer than you!" she yelled.

Dado's face hardened. "How dare you! Clear this table at once, and get on with your homework!"

But Alison ignored her. Abruptly she changed her mind about going out and stomped off upstairs.

"Come back down!"

Alison slammed her bedroom door. At times she hated her aunt – *really* hated her. This was one of them.

Loud steps sounded on the landing. Dado pushed into the room her face flushed with anger. "Don't slam your door on me, madam! I'll not have it. And what's that?"

She stared at a heap lying by the wardrobe. Alison groaned. It was the red knitted dress.

"So *that's* how you treat a lovely birthday present!"

"Lovely?" yelled Alison. "It was *horrid*! And you're a mean old bitch!"

Dado's face turned crimson. Before Alison could move her aunt's hand lashed out and slapped her in the face.

Tears stung Alison's eyes.

"Pick it up. At once!"

It's hard to know why Dado glanced at this moment at the wardrobe. Perhaps a flicker of light in the long mirror. But her mouth fell open in surprise.

Two faces were staring out at her. Her own... and a second, chalk-white.

She swung round to see behind. There was no one there. She stared back at the mirror in disbelief. A ghostly figure of a girl was standing at her side – a girl with dark cropped hair and curious clothes, her face glowing eerily.

Dado's terrified shriek filled the room. She dragged at the bedroom door and stumbled out across the landing.

Alison got to the mirror as the pale figure of Alicia faded into nothingness.

19 – SHATTERING GLASS

Alison woke next morning dreading the moment she and Dado would meet. What would her aunt say? As it was, she was late.

Steps sounded on the landing. Dado was already up and going down the stairs. Alison grabbed her clothes. *Better get to the bus quickly*. She didn't want a row.

The kitchen was empty and she was gulping a glass of milk as Dado came in at the back door, her face gaunt.

Now for it.

To her surprise her aunt was holding a long-handled axe.

Dado said: "What are you still doing here? You're going to miss the bus."

Alison almost answered that she had only just come down but she stopped herself and stared as Dado moved towards the staircase door.

"Get out of my way!"

The woman's mouth seemed to twist sideways.

"But I need my school things," protested Alison.

"Then *get* them!"

Alison raced up the stairs and scooped her books into her school bag. Whatever was happening? Her aunt was looking positively strange.

She hurried back down.

Dado did not wrap it up. "You'll be alone tonight. I'm going to stay at the Marshall's."

"Aunt D, are you all right?"

"Of course I am. And stop staring."

She turned towards the staircase.

Alison waited no longer; she dragged on her shoes, determined to get out of the house as fast as she could. She was half-standing in the hall, still tying her laces as a crash of shattering glass sounded upstairs. A second frightening crash followed the first.

She bounded up, two steps at a time, and halted at her bedroom door. Another crash filled the place.

Dado was hacking the wardrobe to pieces.

"Aunt D!"

"Get out!" yelled the woman.

Alison stood, shocked.

"Get out *now*!"

Dado turned towards her, grasping the axe in both hands.

Alison fled.

*

At school she was in a bad way. She was terrified of going home. She would run away and not come back – that's what she would do! Dado had lost the plot.

She longed to tell Miss Marsden what had happened. The teacher seemed endlessly busy and at home-time disappeared into a staff meeting. It was no good; she would have to find Alicia. She would tell her. She desperately needed to talk.

She got off the bus and stood at the roadside, not wanting to walk the last bit. Rain had started to fall and she felt cold. The house was just visible through the trees. Had Dado already gone? She tried to see if smoke was coming from the chimney but couldn't tell. She waited until long after the sound of the bus engine had died away before she set off along the track.

Her aunt's car wasn't there. Relieved, she entered the kitchen and dumped her bag. The axe was propped against the wall. She put the kettle on and only then did she go upstairs.

The mess in her bedroom was still a shock. The wardrobe lay in pieces, shards of glass glittering among the debris. She looked into Dado's room and backed out quickly: the dresser mirror lay smashed.

Down in the kitchen she heated a tin of spaghetti and turned up the Rayburn until it started to roar. Gradually the warmth helped.

An empty house... She had been alone before, but now it seemed scary and lonely. For a time she put off going back up to her bedroom, but knowing she was being a wimp, she grabbed a brush and dustpan.

She carried the broken pieces of wardrobe down to the kitchen, wondering how to get rid of them. Having no better idea, she opened the back door and threw them into the yard. The crash of wood landing on the cobbles broke the silence. That felt better!

She brushed up the glass and tipped it into a bucket. Broken slivers of wood lay in corners, but they could wait.

Clutching a hot water bottle, she got into bed early and lay there wishing she had gone to look for Alicia. Somehow the girl had become more real than any of the girls at school. First thing in the morning she would try again. She would. She *must.* And there was little Peter – if he really did exist. She feared that in the end Alicia was going to be terribly disappointed.

For a while as she lay there she stared at the shattered base of her wardrobe, and remembered again the look of terror on Dado's face. She fell asleep with the light still on.

20 – HUNTING FOR PETER

Alison slept badly. Daylight came and though it was only six-thirty she couldn't stop in bed a moment longer. She got dressed. Saturday – a new morning. Usually this was her favourite day, but she was unsettled. She made a jam butty and ate it as she went out to the pond.

A gust of wind swept the surface as she paused by the boulder. Of course, the girl would hardly be in the water again.

"Your aunt," said a low voice. "She is not here?"

Out of nowhere Alicia appeared alongside her.

Alison laughed. "I *knew* you'd do that! You like making me jump, don't you?" And then: "She's away till Monday. She's been going crazy and messing up the house…"

She trailed off as she saw Alicia's expression.

"What's the matter?"

Alicia looked deeply unhappy.

"Oh, I'm sorry. It's Peter, isn't it?"

"Perhaps it really is too long ago," confessed the girl.

Alison pointed. "There's those trees at the start of the track. Let's try up there."

She slipped a comforting hand into Alicia's and they walked together.

"The woman," said Alicia.

"You frightened her…"

"I don't trust her."

They stood in among the trees, Alicia pausing to listen. They moved on and a minute later halted and listened again.

She shook her head.

Alison said: "What does Peter look like? How would I know him?"

"You'd soon know. He is small and very cheeky. And he wears awful clothes."

Alison bit at her lip. There was nowhere else she could think of looking. They returned and sat by the ash.

The water shone like a mirror, the house reflected in its shiny surface. Because they were sitting on the far side of the pond its image was upside down, but it was as clear as a picture. It had been one of the first things Alison had sketched.

"I think we've been searching in the wrong place," said Alison suddenly.

Alicia guessed her thoughts. "He won't be inside."

"How can you be sure?"

"I just know. He never liked being indoors. He always wanted to be outside. He even wanted to sleep outside."

A figure came trooping down the track. Alison groaned. It was the postman. "We mustn't give up yet. We must…"

But Alicia vanished.

21 – A TREMOR

The postman left two letters, both addressed to Dado; neither was from the solicitor. Alison, however, had her mind set on something else. She thought for a moment, then decided to go through every part of the house. She set off slowly, knowing she was probably being silly but determined to try. She stood for a full minute in each room. Each time she heard nothing unusual.

Not until she entered the little box bedroom at the top of the house did she have a first strange feeling. It was scarcely anything – a tremor that disappeared the moment it happened.

She stared at a trapdoor above her in the ceiling. It was a lot of bother but she went downstairs for a ladder and got her aunt's torch from her bedroom. Heart thumping, she propped the ladder against the edge of the trap and climbed up.

The loft was full of boxes and abandoned furniture. Heaps of old canvasses lay at one end, while tea chests blocked out the other. She tried listening. At first there was nothing special, but gradually she identified a low creaking. It came from deep down, somewhere far away, as if the house were easing its old bones. Near at hand she was startled to hear scratching. A mouse? But other sounds? Nothing.

She searched through everything, not knowing really what to listen for. It seemed hopeless. She pulled aside the tea chests but there was only a plastered wall; she looked through all the canvasses again.

She was about to climb down the ladder and go outside when she remembered Dado and her hammering. She looked again at the wall. This time she sat on the floorboards and listened. Again there was nothing.

But there was! A distant trembling, something faintly active. A tremor.

Searching the floor, she picked up an old shoe and tapped at the wall where the boxes had been piled. At the far end it sounded hollow.

Using the heel, she hit the wall hard and a piece of plaster split off, then a second piece. A strip of wood began to show.

A dozen hefty blows brought off the rest of the plaster and revealed a small blue door. She was excited now... had she found the missing piece of the will?

Catching the edge of the wood with her nails, she tugged the door open. The shreds of a tattered curtain hung inside, and beyond the faded strands was a little figure. A small boy was sitting on a wooden chair, unmoving, as if carved in stone. Shining.

Alison raced out of the house, calling for Alicia. She had found him! He was in the loft... a little boy!

She called out by the boulder. Alongside the giant ash she called again; the light turned hazy and Alicia was at her side.

"It's Peter! I've found him!"

Alicia looked stunned.

"He's in the loft!"

"In the house?"

"Yes, yes! In the house!"

They raced up the stairs, struggled up the ladder and halted breathlessly in the loft. The little figure was still there in the recess, half hidden behind the curtain, shining in the gloom, his eyes closed.

A little ghost boy.

22 – A WILD ONE

Alicia tore the curtain shreds aside.

"Peter! Oh, Peter!"

Her face was bright. She touched him on the cheek. A flickering bluish light filled the tiny cupboard and slowly the boy's eyes opened. At the same time his white statue-like appearance eased until a small boy was sitting there, transformed, with cherubic cheeks and dark curly hair. He was smooth-skinned and barefooted, his clothes rough homespun: a pair of worn breeches and a worn jacket.

"Oh, he's beautiful," said Alison.

"He is *perfect*," whispered Alicia. She took him in her arms.

Alison listened as Alicia quietly cooed, and then there was an unexpected sound. A chuckle. No, not a chuckle – Peter was clearing his throat.

Alison studied the boy's face. His eyes were a startling blue. They were shining and full of mischief.

"It's me!" he said, his voice grating. And then more clearly: "It's me!"

They went down – down the loft ladder, down the stairs, down into the world outside.

Alison was full of excitement but she held back, waiting by the farmhouse door to let them be on their own. Excited talk filled the afternoon and then Alison was startled by a sudden change of tone. Alicia seemed to be scolding the boy! She was stamping her foot and grabbing at him, and he raced off.

"Come back!" she yelled. "Come back or I'll spank you!"

But Little Peter jumped around, waving his arms excitedly, and dodged her attempts to seize hold.

"He's a little terror!" exclaimed Alicia as Alison hurried over. "He's not changed one bit and... *got you*!" She grabbed behind her as the boy came too close.

"Now stop it at once!"

"I won't, I won't!" laughed Peter. He tweaked her nose with his fingers and wriggled madly.

Alicia held him tightly and grinned. "He's always been a wild one!"

She turned to him. "And just what were you doing in the cupboard? Fast asleep?"

His face shone. "I was hiding. You were hiding, so I was hiding too!"

"I wasn't hiding at all," said Alicia, but she said no more and gave him a wild squeeze.

Alison marvelled. Had he been sitting on that little chair through all the years? All alone? It seemed so. No wonder he wanted to charge around! She was astonished too at the sudden change in Alicia. She was no longer the quiet solemn figure she had come to know. Her face, as white as ever, shone with happiness as she clutched her squirming little brother. Little? He seemed a dynamo!

"Can I help?"

Unwittingly Alison got too near, then yelled as Little Peter grabbed her hair and tugged excitedly.

"Ow! Stop! Don't!"

Between them the girls got him to let go. At once he tried to scramble away.

Alicia had had enough. She grabbed him by his legs and tipped him up off the ground.

"Stop it!" she ordered, holding him by the ankles. "Or you can stay upside down."

The boy yelled in protest.

She shook him hard. "Are you going to behave?"

"Yes, yes!"

"Promise?"

"I promise!"

She turned him the right way up but did not let go.

"Brothers," she groaned.

Slowly she began to look more composed.

"He's so quick. Just like old times!"

Alison laughed. He was certainly a wild one.

"He'll run off again!"

"Not while I have hold of him."

"I've been keeping watch over you all!" yelled Peter. "For years and years."

"Playing, you mean." said Alicia.

Still clutching him she turned towards the pond. It took several moments before Alison realised what was happening.

"Wait, what are you doing?"

They were approaching the edge.

"It is time to leave," said Alicia.

This took Alison by surprise.

"Oh you mustn't go," she cried, dismayed. "You can't!"

But Alicia was no longer laughing. Her arms still locked round the boy, she paused as if trying to decide what to say.

"We are sisters!" said Alison. "That's what you said."

The other girl looked at her solemnly.

Alison was desperate. "You can stay with me, here in the house. Both of you – I'll find a way. I will. I promise. And we could play at magic lights. The three of us. Oh, please!"

Alicia looked down at little Peter. It seemed as if she were never going to speak.

"There is a way," she said at last. She spoke slowly. "But only if you really want... only if... if you leave everything."

Her voice had become very quiet. "You could step down into my world with me..."

She paused as if to let the thought take hold.

"... then we could always be together," she said softly.

Alison began to tremble. For a wild moment she almost said she would do it, she would go with her, but she held back and, hardly seconds, the moment passed. It was no use. She knew she dared not.

"I can't," she said.

Alicia smiled. "Our two worlds…"

"The sun and the moon," said Alison.

"Yes," said Alicia, "the sun and the moon. But you must not be sad; we'll always remember each other. I know we will."

She half turned. "You must see behind the face," she said softly.

Alison didn't understand, but there was no time to say more. Alicia took firmer hold of the boy and stepped into the pond. She moved in slowly, the water rising up until it covered the boy and reached her shoulders. For a moment she paused, caught in the glittering surface, then she took another step and disappeared.

The water turned into a shining mirror.

Tears stung Alison's eyes. She had so wanted Alicia to be the sister she'd never had, and for a time that was how it seemed it might be. But now, no matter how much she wished that to happen, it never would. Dear Alicia! More than anything she had so wanted to find Little Peter, and now she had. Alison knew she would have felt the same.

23 – ACCIDENT

Monday passed and Alison arrived home from school and rarely had she felt so lonely. The kitchen door was ajar so Dado was around somewhere. A fresh patch of broken plaster lay strewn outside the pantry floor. Her crazy aunt was still hunting for the will! Yet there was no hideaway, no hidden cupboard except the one in the loft that she had uncovered, and the will had certainly not been in there.

She went into the hall and was shocked to find the painting of her grandfather, the whiskery one, dumped on the floor with the glass cracked. The wall behind it had been chiselled, exposing more stonework. Books had been pulled off the shelves and left in heaps. Even her dad's old note book. Angrily she grabbed it up. *I'll run away*, she vowed. *I will. I will.*

She hurried up the stairs. She would grab her things. She would go *now*. Anywhere.

Dado's bedroom door was shut and without knowing why Alison paused outside to listen. Now that she thought about it, the house was strangely quiet as if something were about to happen. Well she would run away, that's what would happen.

She grasped the handle of the door, not really wanting to look inside; yet aware that she was being silly, and it would not matter, she pushed the door open.

She stood petrified.

Dado lay on the floor in a heap. For a moment Alison thought she was unconscious, but her aunt gave a low groan and opened her eyes. She had been crying.

"Oh, thank goodness you're here," she gasped.

"Aunt D! What's happened?"

"My ankle. I think it's broken."

Dado's right leg was twisted beneath her.

"The box gave way."

Alison took hold of her hand. She could see what had happened: Dado had been standing on a box as she hammered at the wall but the wood had split under her weight.

"Can you move at all, just a little? If I put my arm under yours can you get up onto the bed?"

But Dado couldn't. It was too painful. Alison realised she needed help. She eased a pillow under

Dado's head, raced downstairs, found a bottle of painkillers and gave her two tablets.

"I'll go for help."

Dado's face was drawn. "The Walkers?"

"I'll get them."

She ran from the house. She didn't stop running until she reached Walkers' farm down the road and banged at their door and called desperately for someone to come.

24 – A DISASTROUS WILL

It was half-term and everything had changed. Alison sat at the kitchen table, and using a dry cloth she wiped the dust off her father's old notebook. It was generously thick and the cover was stained with a brown ring where a mug of tea had once rested, but inside the book the pages were undamaged and covered in a mass of tiny drawings. Sketches of chimney pots and birds, a sheep dog, a fence, trees, ragged clouds. She loved them all and went on turning the pages until she came to the middle. And then she stopped and looked no further.

The door rattled and the dumpy figure of Aunt Betty came in, laden with bags of shopping.

"Phew. Sorry. What a rush. Got to the hospital and I managed to see Dado, then got the shopping. Parking a nightmare. But good news, she's definitely a bit better. I hadn't realised till now how bad a break it was: a multiple fracture. A doctor told me it was going to take quite a time but he thinks it will probably be all right in the end if she take things quietly."

She dumped everything, her face bright and cheery.

"So that's good. Now surprise me, I don't suppose you are hungry? *You are?* How extraordinary. Then let's get the kettle on."

Alison grinned. Suddenly Cobbles Farm felt a happy home again. The little aunt's presence had changed everything.

"Let's have lasagna."

But Alison was itching to show her the notebook. "No, Aunt B. Wait. I've something to show you. Something special."

She spread the book on the table. The open pages in the middle took a second to register. It was the third piece of the will.

"Well I never!" The little woman was astonished. "Trust your clever dad. Goodness, shall I phone? Yes, I will. Now where's my mobile? Goodness me. How brilliant!"

She rummaged in her handbag and beamed. "I'll call right away."

Alison laughed. She was so happy. Betty had agreed to stay, though only for two more weeks. After that there would be a problem.

Alison found the lasagna while Betty phoned the solicitor and got them an appointment for two o'clock. Then Alison wrapped up the notebook.

A thought was bothering her. "What if Aunt Dado doesn't come back? I mean, can't you stay? You know, for more than just two weeks?"

Aunt Betty's face became serious. "Deary me, I'm afraid I can't. I'll have to go back home eventually, my dear. Really the will does not involve me; but don't let's worry about that just now. See, I've bought two vanilla slices for pudding. Big ones. Now we must hurry – we'll have to be away in an hour."

At two minutes to two Betty reversed her Volvo into a parking slot in Newtown, with just the slightest bump into the car behind.

"I'm definitely going to get a motorbike. This Volvo's getting too big for me, though I love it."

"Some motorbikes can be big, too. A bit like armchairs."

"I'll get a Honda. A little C50."

Alison was no wiser.

They hurried up the steps into the solicitor's offices and were shown into Mr Wilkinson's room.

Alison introduced her Aunt Betty. Mr Wilkinson said he was very sorry about Miss Dado but glad she was being cared for and hoped her broken ankle would soon mend.

And then Alison produced the parcel.

The solicitor sat forward. "So you really *have* found the third part of the will?"

"I'll show you," said Alison.

She undid the wrapping and placed her father's shabby notebook on the desk.

"Look in the middle."

Mr Wilkinson turned the pages. "It is tucked inside?"

Alison glanced at her aunt and they smiled. "You must keep turning."

Chimney pots, birds, a sheep dog, a fence, trees and clouds, hens pecking in the dust…

And then he found the missing part of the will. Part Three had been stuck across the two middle pages. It was decorated with drawings of swooping swallows, and trees, and cats with twisted tails. The text was written clearly.

"Goodness!" exclaimed the solicitor.

"Dad had lots of notebooks but this was his special one. He drew things all the time."

"So he did." Mr Wilkinson turned the pages eagerly but as he went on through them his excitement slowly evaporated.

"Deary me, I confess I had been hoping for more than just the missing piece."

There was nothing else. Certainly no copy of a complete will.

He produced the first two zigzag parts and placed them on the open notebook. All three fitted together perfectly.

But Mr Wilkinson was no happier. "It's as I feared. We are no better off. I'm afraid the probate court will not accept this, er... this document. You must read it all for yourselves."

THE WILL AND TESTAMENT
of
ANDREW AND MARY BENSON
Until she is 21, Alison Benson at
the property Cobbles Farm
Shall be occupied by her
under the GUIDANCE of a
Guardian D Fletcher,
of Newtown

To D Fletcher we entrust
a Third of this Will document
to her care
With the sum of £5,000
while so caring
She will also Receive an Allowance
to be Determined by
J L Wilkinson and Drone
the aforesaid
solicitors for as long as she takes
Good care of
The before mentioned
Alison Benson.

Added across the foot of the page lay the third piece of the will:

Should all circumstances
be in order then our Daughter
Alison Benson
shall inherit Cobbles Farm
in total when she is
Twenty-One years of age
and able to manage the Estate

in Her Own Right.

Aunt Betty said hopefully: "It does seem to be all right. It says the farm will be Alison's."

The solicitor shook his head. "Sadly, that is not the problem. As I explained to Miss Dado I expected to find a modern will along with this third piece. Perhaps concealed in a secret place in the house?"

He adjusted his glasses. "As it is, I have checked the law and wills have to be undamaged in order to be legal. A tear, or even a hole in a page, and certainly an old one like this in pieces, can mean a lot of difficulty."

"But it does say the house will be mine," said Alison.

The solicitor became cautious. "Yes, if the will were legal. But I fear the probate court will rule this document is invalid."

He looked sympathetically at Alison. "What we need is a proper modern will. I am surprised one does not exist."

Alison and Aunt Betty exchanged glances.

"Perhaps one does?" said Betty, hopefully.

Mr Wilkinson frowned. "I would have thought my associate, the late Mr Drone, would have suggested there should be one. It is certainly a little strange."

"What can we do?" Betty asked.

"I'll have the staff search the file rooms again. Meanwhile there is the problem of Miss Dado – that is to say Miss Fletcher – I wonder just how poorly she is. Will she be able to manage the house any longer?"

He turned inquiringly to Aunt Betty.

"She is getting better," Betty told him. "But she has mentioned about moving into a flat. She seems to be changing her mind about being at Cobbles Farm."

Mr Wilkinson explained about executors and guardians, and how complicated it was going to be to sort out the will.

Alison stopped listening. She fitted the strips together again. Dad had often done things in a funny way. She remembered the terrible morning he'd tried to burn all his paintings, saying they were badly painted and he was getting nowhere. He'd piled the canvasses in the yard, but before he could set them ablaze it had started pouring with rain. Alison and her mother had raced to carry the pictures back indoors and despite his protests eventually re-hung them – even the ones where rain had caused runny streaks.

Alison came to something and read it twice.

"Mr Wilkinson!" She broke in excitedly. "It says *D Fletcher* is my guardian!"

Both grown-ups looked puzzled.

"Well, don't you see? That could be Aunt Betty! She's D Fletcher, too, only she's *Delia* Fletcher. They're *both* D Fletcher!"

Aunt Betty looked surprised.

Alison was bursting with excitement. "So Aunt Betty could stay. I mean, if she wants to?"

She broke off.

Betty shook her head. "I never use my real name."

"But you are D Fletcher!"

Mr Wilkinson reread the text and glanced approvingly at Alison. "Well spotted. You are quite right. This wording is ambiguous – something I should have noticed myself. Undoubtedly the names should have been spelled out in full. Normally that is the case; sadly it does not help all that much as I fear the will still won't be legal."

He took off his glasses and wiped them with a tissue.

"I must find a way to deal with this. I shall contact you again shortly."

There seemed little more to say. Alison and Betty left feeling gloomy. The strange will seemed to be a disaster.

*

Next day they blitzed the house. They mopped it from top to bottom, determined to get rid of the dust. The work did Alison good. Since the scary moment when she had found Dado lying on the floor she felt a great deal older than twelve.

She rescued her grandfather's painting from the hall floor. She laid the frame on the kitchen table and they picked out fragments of broken glass.

"We'll easily get a new piece cut," said Betty. "It's a miracle the picture is still in one piece."

Alison stared at the old man's whiskery face. It was a self-portrait. He wore a white wing collar and looked very old fashioned but it was a clever painting. When people went past it his eyes seemed to follow them. Her dad used to say he was making sure he was keeping an eye on everything.

Then Alison went cold with excitement. The face. *Behind the face.* She had suddenly remembered Alicia's last words. She stared into her grandfather's eyes.

"Aunt Betty, turn it over."

She did not explain. She tore a layer of paper off the back of the frame.

A buff envelope tumbled out.

"Oh, Aunt B, I know what it is!" she cried excitedly.

The envelope was fat and sealed with a blob of red wax.

25 – BETTY HAS TO DECIDE

Alison and Betty arrived at the solicitors and an intrigued Mr Wilkinson broke open the seal. At once he looked happier. Inside the fat envelope was a folded, typed legal document. It made everything clear. Cobbles Farm would become Alison's when she was twenty-one.

Mr Wilkinson shuffled the papers. "Excellent, excellent. That is a relief. Now it brings me to another important matter."

He looked meaningfully at Aunt Betty.

"I have received a letter from Miss Dado in which she says that for health and other unspecified reasons, she has regretfully decided she no longer wishes to live at Cobbles Farm. Indeed, she has been advised to take things more quietly even if it means giving up looking after Alison. Apparently she is suffering from shock, no doubt from the fall.

"Therefore, I wonder, subject to the necessary legal procedures – I wonder if perhaps you yourself might be able to help at Cobbles Farm? Like in the past weeks?"

Betty looked surprised.

"Obviously," he went on, "Alison can't live alone, but there is a weekly allowance and if you were able to step in and assume the responsibility of running everything then that would be a perfect solution. Permanently, that is."

Alison was trembling. "Oh, Aunt Betty, will you?"

For the first time chubby Betty looked flustered. She was doing her best to think. "Deary me, I confess it has crossed my mind several times, wondering how I might be able to help, but of course the will does not mention me. Not really. And such a big change... I mean, all my furniture, and then living in the country. I'm a town person really."

Alison's face lit with enthusiasm. "You'd soon be a country lady, Aunt Betty, I know you would. I'd help you become one. You're becoming one now!"

Mr Wilkinson and Betty laughed.

Alison went on: "Please say you will, Aunt Betty. And the will does mention you – you *are* D Fletcher. I mean you do like Cobbles Farm don't you?"

Betty's cheeks seemed to go even pinker. "Of course I do. It's just I have always lived by myself."

"Then say yes," begged Alison. *"Please."*

Betty glanced at Mr Wilkinson as if hoping he would help her to decide, and then she looked at the expression on Alison's face. For a moment no one spoke. Then Betty decided. "If that's what you want, then yes, of course I will. Why not! If you really want me? I think it would be wonderful."

Alison threw herself into Betty's arms.

"I'll never be late for school," cried Alison. "And I'll always look after my clothes, and I'll not catch colds in the rain and…"

"Goodness!" laughed Betty. "I hope you are not going to be a boring perfect child."

They left the solicitor's office, Alison overflowing with happiness. As they went down the steps Betty said it was time for a cup of tea, and being a towny person she knew a perfect café at the end of the street where they sold giant slices of jam sponge cake.

"Very fattening. But even if we live at Cobbles we'll come into town often because there are lots of cafés, and in any case I might buy a motorbike."

"Then I'll ride on the back seat," promised Alison.

They had a sumptuous afternoon tea, then Betty took extra care and got out of the parking slot bump free.

"I've been thinking very seriously," she said. "If you agree, we must make a few changes at Cobbles."

Alison felt a pang of alarm. She remembered Dado's changes.

"We must get you a mobile phone. How you manage without one I don't know. And there's no telly. You must be the only girl in school without a telly. We must get a telly if only to watch the football."

No, Alison decided, Betty and Dado were nowhere near alike. The thought prompted another idea.

She told Betty.

The little woman nodded. "Of course I will. What about right now?"

"Please," said Alison.

Betty stayed in the car while Alison entered Newtown Hospital. A nurse pointed to a bed down the ward.

Dado was propped upright on the pillows, her left leg stretched out, encased in plaster. She looked pink and calm.

"What a nice surprise," she said as she saw Alison. Her voice had lost its edge and had become relaxed. It was not at all like the cross sound of the past.

"I'm so sorry you're in hospital," said Alison. "I hope you're feeling a bit better."

"Yes, I am, thank you. I was so lucky you came when you did."

Alison produced a box. "I've brought you some liquorish allsorts."

A woman arrived and placed a jug of water on the bedside chest.

Dado waited until she had gone. "Liquorish allsorts? I love them! How ever did you know? But more important, how is Betty coping? She's been to see me and I hope you are both managing. She can be a bit dotty at times."

"She's helping a lot."

Dado sighed. "The doctor has insisted that I must take things easy. So I expect you know I'll not be coming back after all. I'm really sorry. As it is, I've been found a little flat here in Newtown where I plan to live. One that's easy to manage."

"Then I'll come and see you," promised Alison.

She sat while Dado explained that it was a complicated break and she had been very lucky Alison had found her in time. Her ankle might never be perfect again but she was doing her best and knew she was going to have to manage. She said again she was sorry she would no longer be able to act as Alison's guardian.

No mention was made of the mirror in the wardrobe.

Alison gave her aunt a kiss. "I'll come and see you tomorrow," she promised.

26 – NEVER MORE BEAUTIFUL

At first Alison sat outside on the boulder and did her homework, hoping each day that she would catch a glimpse of Alicia. But it was a forlorn hope and the more time that passed the more she began to feel it was not going to happen. The pond lay sunlit and unruffled. More irises had opened their yellow flowers and never had the water looked more beautiful. Yet its beauty was lost on her.

If only she could do something to make Alicia appear! She remembered the first time they'd met. Perhaps Alicia couldn't return even if she wanted to; perhaps she was trapped again just like then.

As the days went by she sat by the pond less often, preferring to write indoors out of the bright light. There seemed lots of other things to do. The weather was brilliant, the sun blazing in a vault-like sky. At day end, she raced to do her homework, and then she joined Aunt Betty in the Volvo and off they went, touring the villages beyond Newtown. Twice, as a treat, they ate at small pubs and in this way the days passed and Alison did not notice the change that was taking place in the pond not, that is, until one Saturday morning.

She sat on the big boulder and rubbed her face and limbs with suntan cream. She took off her socks and shoes and laid them on the bank. She propped herself on the rock and let her feet reach down into the cool water, where they sent little circles eddying out into the glare. But it was too hot to stay for long. She rose to leave and it was now that a worrying thought struck her. She set a twig in the mud at the edge of the bank to test it.

Several days passed before she checked the twig again, and even in that short time the water had gone down a little. She set another twig and the next time she looked it was lower still. Dismayed, she realised that the pond was beginning to shrink.

Alison listened to the weather forecasts on the radio. They were full of drought warnings. What would happen if the pond shrank away altogether? It was a frightening thought. Alison told herself it just never would.

But the thought persisted. It was not impossible. What would happen to Alicia and

Peter if the pond dried up? Had it ever happened before?

In desperation she went to the garden shed and dragged out the hosepipe. She connected it to the tap in the kitchen and laid it through the hall and out the front door.

Betty looked at it. "Are you watering the garden?"

"It's the pond, said Alison. "It's shrinking."

Her aunt came out to look. "I'm afraid you're right. Better give it a good long run."

But the hosepipe did not reach the pond; it was three metres short. Alison turned on the water and tried filling a bucket from the hose end. She carried the bucket the last few metres and tipped it in. But it was hard work and after struggling with six full buckets she gave up.

Aunt Betty helped her search through the junk in the garden shed, and they found a yellow plastic hose. It was old and cracked but it might do. They bound the two hose ends together with sticky tape and now the pipe reached the pond. It leaked, but water began to run through. Feeling more optimistic, Alison left it running all day, and at Betty's suggestion, all night too.

Come morning, Alison was almost in tears. The pond looked no better. The last marker twig in the mud was still above the water line.

Though Betty was curious about Alison's behaviour she didn't ask questions. All she said was: "It will surely rain again eventually."

Alison nodded.

Should she tell Aunt Betty the real reason for her concern? She hesitated: perhaps her aunt would laugh. She would certainly be surprised if she saw a ghost girl.

And then, finally, one day there came a distant rumble. At first Alison thought it was plane passing high overhead, but a second rumble came and she realised excitedly that it was thunder. More rumbling came from the south and now that she looked harder, she could see a faint haziness.

She stood at the pond's edge. *Come on, come on*, she thought, *why don't you rain?*

The haze grew darker and at last she could see real clouds. It seemed to take forever for them to creep north.

Finally the rain came in the night, and the noise woke her. Joyfully she tumbled out of bed and rushed across the room. She opened the window and rain poured in. It was tremendous. She couldn't have felt happier. Only when she was soaked did she close the windows and put on dry pyjamas.

She was out early next morning, and how everything had changed! The pond was full. What must it have been like for Alicia as the night skies had emptied into her world? If only she would appear and they could talk.

Then a wild idea struck her. Why didn't she try to *make* her appear? Aunt Betty was still in the house; it was all clear.

For a moment she dithered and then: "A fine friend you are!" she shouted.

The water swallowed her voice.

"I know you can hear me!" she yelled loudly. "Don't think I don't!"

She didn't know at all, but what did that matter?

"Why don't you come back?" she pleaded.

There was a lull, during which not even a bird could be heard.

"I hate you! I hate you! I hate you!" she yelled.

The sun was growing hotter. Alison flopped down against the big stone. She didn't know why she kept trying to see her. Nothing seemed the same any more.

And then she saw something move.

Down in the shining depths, Alicia and little Peter were beginning to appear. Their ghostly figures wavered, half-seen, as if the water were swirling. It lasted for several moments and then it, steadied and now she could see them clearly, side by side.

Alison hardly dared to breathe. She knelt on the bank. It was almost like the first day they'd met. But what would happen if she did the same as then? Would she be grabbed? Dare she risk it?

She stretched a hand out over the water and at once there was a movement. Alison's heart missed a beat. Alicia had seen her. She was reaching towards the surface.

Where water ended and sky began, the tips of their fingers touched.

Sisters, thought Alison.

A familiar trembling sensation swept through her. Ripples spread across the water in bright circles, as if they were messengers, then seemingly from nowhere a soft voice sifted in among her thoughts: *Like the sun…* it whispered.

Alison gasped.

…like the moon.

Neither girl moved. The sun was warm. Their fingers were still touching as the light dissolved into an underwater world. And suddenly Alison was no longer crouching on the bank at the edge of the pond. Astonished, she realised she was flowing along in a shining current with Alicia on one side and little Peter on the other. Down they sank, turning in a slow spiral. Minnows came up, staring, and raced away; a spotted belly newt fan-tailed out of sight. Small green lagoons opened, one behind the other, in among the iris stems.

Alison gave a shiver. A host of vague faces had appeared around her. They were white and hazy, their eyes shimmering softly as if watching.

Now you see my world. Our world, said Alicia's soft voice. *All those who have lived by the water.*

For long eerie seconds the faces hovered without moving, then slowly they faded.

*

High overhead the sun grew brighter and turned the pond into a shining mirror. The girls' fingers parted, and now it was Alicia who faded from sight, lost in the brightness.

Alison jerked upright. Oh! She was sitting on the bank against the boulder. Had she been swimming alongside Alicia… or was it a dream, it had been so vivid. She stood up and looked into the depths of the water. It shone wonderfully.

I'll see you again Alicia, she whispered. *I'm sure I'll see you again.*

Hot though the sun was her clothes were still wet and dripping to the ground.

Alison felt immensely happy. She knew now something she had not known an hour ago: she would always be able to find Alicia. She would always be there. The water guarded their secret.

It was an important moment, a moment that was to change everything. Alison ran into the house and fetched a notebook and pencil. She would start again. She must draw her friend's face quickly while she remembered it. Working swiftly, in bold strokes, she felt inspired. It seemed to take no time before she held up Alicia's portrait.

It was a good likeness; she hadn't realised she could draw this well. She laid the picture on the boulder and placed small pebbles on its edges to stop it blowing away. Tomorrow she would frame it and hang it in the hallway, and she would tell Aunt Betty the girl's name. Perhaps she would tell her everything.

But drawing Alicia's picture was not all. There was something else she had to draw, something she remembered from long ago – something important.

Picking up the notebook, she stared up at the sky. *Light*. She would draw *Light*. Somehow, deep down, she knew she could do it.

And she knew now what she was going to be.

#0147 - 250616 - C0 - 210/148/8 - PB - DID1495758